1853

TROUBLES FOR
Cécile

By DENISE LEWIS PATRICK

ILLUSTRATIONS CHRISTINE KORNACKI

VIGNETTES CINDY SALANS ROSENHEIM

☆AmericanGirl®

THE AMERICAN GIRLS

1764

KAYA, an adventurous Nez Perce girl whose deep love for horses and respect for nature nourish her spirit

1774

FELICITY, a spunky, spritely colonial girl, full of energy and independence

1824

JOSEFINA, a Hispanic girl whose heart and hopes are as big as the New Mexico sky

1853

CÉCILE AND MARIE-GRACE, two girls whose friendship helps them—and New Orleans— survive terrible times

1854

KIRSTEN, a pioneer girl of strength and spirit who settles on the frontier

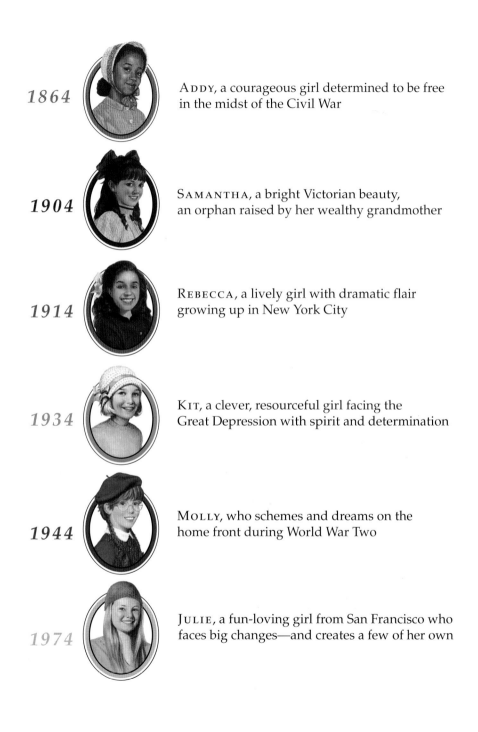

1864 ADDY, a courageous girl determined to be free in the midst of the Civil War

1904 SAMANTHA, a bright Victorian beauty, an orphan raised by her wealthy grandmother

1914 REBECCA, a lively girl with dramatic flair growing up in New York City

1934 KIT, a clever, resourceful girl facing the Great Depression with spirit and determination

1944 MOLLY, who schemes and dreams on the home front during World War Two

1974 JULIE, a fun-loving girl from San Francisco who faces big changes—and creates a few of her own

Questions or comments? Call 1-800-845-0005, visit **americangirl.com**,
or write to Customer Service, American Girl, 8400 Fairway Place,
Middleton, WI 53562-0497.

Printed in China
11 12 13 14 15 16 LEO 10 9 8 7 6 5 4 3 2 1

Profound appreciation to Mary Niall Mitchell, Associate Professor of History,
University of New Orleans; Sally Kittredge Reeves, former Notarial Archivist, New Orleans;
and Thomas A. Klingler, Associate Professor, Dept. of French and Italian, Tulane University.

PICTURE CREDITS
The following individuals and organizations have generously
given permission to reprint images contained in "Looking Back":
p. 75—photograph by Tess Conrad; pp. 76–77—orphanage scene, © Bettmann/Corbis;
mosquito, photograph by Steven Doggett; Philadelphia epidemic scene, © Bettmann/Corbis;
pp. 78–79—sick boy, courtesy of the Collections of Louisiana State Museum; portrait of James
O'Regan, The Historic New Orleans Collection, accessions no. 2009.0159 MSS 590, F. 10 (detail);
letter, The Historic New Orleans Collection, accessions no. 2009.0159 MSS 590, F. 25, P. 1 (detail);
Charity Hospital ward, Wisconsin Historical Society, WHi-74505; pp. 80–81—burning tar,
North Wind Picture Archives; portrait of Aimée Potens, courtesy of the Roudanez family;
New Orleans cemetery, courtesy of Robert Florence.

Cataloging-in-Publication Data available from the Library of Congress

FOR ALL BRAVE LITTLE GIRLS
WHO GROW UP TO BE
STRONG WOMEN

Cécile and her family speak both
English and French, just as many
people from New Orleans did.
You'll see some French words in this
book. For help in pronouncing or
understanding the foreign words,
look in the glossary on page 82.

TABLE OF CONTENTS

PAPA
Cécile's father, a warm, gentle man and a successful sculptor

MAMAN
Cécile's mother, who is firm but kind and is a good businesswoman

CÉCILE
A confident, curious girl who loves the limelight

ARMAND
Cécile's older brother, who has been studying in Paris, France

GRAND-PÈRE
Cécile's loving grandfather, a retired sailor with many tales to tell

**TANTE OCTAVIA
AND RENÉ**
*Maman's widowed sister
and her son, who live
with Cécile's family*

**MADEMOISELLE
OCÉANE**
*A young opera singer
who gives voice lessons*

MARIE-GRACE
*Cécile's new friend,
who has just moved
back to New Orleans
after several years away*

MATHILDE
*The Reys' housekeeper
and cook*

ELLEN
The Reys' housemaid

CHAPTER
ONE

WHISPERS

July 1853
A fly landed on Cécile's nose.
It tickled. She tried very hard to
ignore it, but she couldn't. She
raised her hand to scratch.

"Cécé! I can't paint your portrait if you don't
sit still," her brother, Armand, warned good-naturedly.

Cécile was wearing her favorite summer dress—
pale cotton with daisies embroidered all over it. Bending
gently over her head were the sweet, butterfly-shaped
flowers of a ginger lily. She was doing her very best
to be a good model as she sat on a stiff chair in the
courtyard of their home on Dumaine Street. But she
was dying to see her brother's work.

"Please, Armand, can't I see what I look like?" she begged.

Armand squinted at the large canvas on the easel in front of him and then winked at his sister. "Ah, *oui*. You can take just a quick peek," he agreed, and Cécile eagerly hopped off the chair. "Promise you won't tell Maman anything about the painting, though. I want to surprise her."

Cécile grinned. She was very good at keeping secrets, and Armand knew it. He had even shared his true dream with Cécile: although he was now working at their father's stonecutting business, he wanted to become a painter, not a stonemason as Papa hoped. This was a truly important secret, because Armand hadn't yet figured out how to explain his feelings to Papa.

Cécile hurried to her brother's side, being careful to hold her skirt away from his paints and brushes. She peered up at the painting.

"Oh! I'm beautiful," she gasped, throwing her arms around his neck.

Armand laughed, and for a moment they studied the half-finished painting together. He had completed only Cécile's golden brown face, but already he seemed to have captured her spirit: her hazel eyes somehow sparkled, and her chin was tilted playfully.

"I'm sure Papa and Maman will be impressed with what a fine painter you are," Cécile began. "Maybe Papa will even—"

"*Shhh!*" Armand put a finger to his lips and glanced toward an open window. His head was tipped as if he was listening to something.

Cécile was surprised to hear her mother's voice drifting outside from the parlor. She thought Maman had already gone out on her errands.

"Octavia, *chérie*, you worry yourself too much." Maman spoke in her usual calm tone, but now Cécile was curious, too. What was worrying Maman's sister, Tante Octavia?

"Aurélia, now the newspapers are reporting that it's yellow fever!" Tante Tay sounded upset. Cécile and Armand looked at each other.

"Remember," Maman went on in a soothing voice, "we were born here in New Orleans. You know that newcomers are always in the greatest danger if yellow fever spreads. But we grew up here. Our family should be safe."

even came to ask Dr. Gardner about the baby!"

Armand looked up at her sharply, as if she were telling the most fantastic tale. His paintbrush froze in the air, dripping on his trousers.

"*C'est vrai!* It's true!" Cécile rushed on with her story. "I asked Tante Tay for some of René's baby clothes, and we dressed Philip in them. Marie-Grace took him to Holy Trinity Orphanage, because her father said no slave catcher would look for him in the orphanage for white children. So now Philip is safe, and even if he *was* born a slave, we'll never tell!"

She stopped to take a breath. Armand stared at her with his mouth open. Cécile wondered nervously if he would say that what she'd done was wrong. She knew that helping slaves escape was against the law.

"I—we—we thought it was the right thing to do," she whispered.

Finally, Armand spoke quietly. "You and Marie-Grace did a brave thing, Cécé. Most people would have been too afraid." He smiled at her. "You have a strong heart, Cécile."

She was startled that her brother hadn't called her by her playful nickname. That meant he was serious, and she felt a flash of pride.

Armand folded his arms and stared at her thoughtfully. "And you're right, Cécile—you're old enough to know what's going on. There's been talk around the city that many people are getting sick with yellow fever, and today the newspapers reported it, too." He paused for a moment. "I know I said that there are some cases in New Orleans every year, but this summer—"

"This summer what?" Cécile leaned forward.

"This summer it may be much worse than that," Armand said. "Some years, hundreds of people get sick. Even thousands. Then it's called an epidemic."

"And, if so many people get yellow fever . . ." Cécile looked straight into her brother's eyes.

Armand nodded slowly. "Many will die. That's what people are afraid of now. No one knows what may come."

"But Maman isn't worried," Cécile said.

Armand nodded again. "Maman isn't worried," he repeated. "Now, let me get some work done on your beautiful portrait before she comes back."

Cécile felt an odd fluttering in the bottom of her stomach, but she reminded herself of her mother's calm, steady words. *We are safe,* she told herself.

Taking a deep breath, she tilted her chin and smiled, just as Armand had posed her before.

The very next Sunday afternoon, Cécile skipped beside her brother and her little cousin, René, at the park on the shores of Lake Pontchartrain, just outside the city. The cool breeze off the water made the park perfect for a picnic under the trees, and everyone in the Rey household had come to enjoy it.

"How I did miss all this when I was away in France!" Armand swept his hat into the air with one long arm, and the picnic basket he was holding in the other hand swung dangerously.

"Didn't you picnic in Paris?" Cécile asked.

"Yes, but with only a hungry memory of Maman's watermelon pickles and Mathilde's tea cakes," he said, lowering the basket carefully, for those precious goodies were inside it. He knelt to check them.

Still smiling, Cécile squinted against the sun. "Look! Papa has already found a picnic spot," she said, pointing up ahead to where her father and Grand-père were spreading a blanket under a shady

"Look, Papa has already found a picnic spot!" Cécile said.

tree. Beside them, Maman was busy gesturing to their young housemaid, Ellen, and Tante Tay was helping Mathilde, the cook, unpack a basket. René scampered off to join the grown-ups.

Armand rose and shrugged as he adjusted his hat. "There seem to be plenty of good picnic spots left."

"You're right," Cécile said, looking around. Scattered here and there were other family groups and clusters of friends, and a train had just pulled to a stop to let its passengers spill out. But the popular park did seem quiet for such a beautiful Sunday afternoon.

"Where is everybody?" Cécile wondered out loud. Then her eyes met her brother's. "You don't think it's because of yellow fever, do you?"

"Now, Cécé." Armand shook his head and spoke in his big-brother tone. "Don't let your imagination carry you away. Lots of families leave New Orleans for the summer. You know that."

Cécile knew that very well. She thought of reminding Armand that she also knew arithmetic very well and that today she could count the number of families sprinkled in the park.

"Put it out of your mind," Armand told her.

"We're here for fun. Look who's gotten off the train!"

Cécile turned to see Monette Bruiller waving. She grinned and waved back. Like Cécile, Monette didn't have sisters, so they always enjoyed each other's company.

Cécile ran to join her friend. "Monette! *Bonjour.*"

"Bonjour, Cécile. I'm so glad to see you!" Monette smiled brightly, and the two girls began to stroll arm in arm. Armand swerved around them, hurrying to deliver his picnic basket so that he could join the noisy clump of Bruiller brothers.

"I haven't seen your brother since he came back from Paris," Monette said. "He is *très gentil.* Very nice!"

Cécile made a face, and Monette laughed. "But he's so handsome—not skinny like my brothers!"

"*Shhh!* Don't tell him that," Cécile joked. Suddenly the boys let out a loud cheer and ran together toward an open area between the trees. "Look! What are they doing?"

"Oh, they're starting a *raquettes* game," Monette said, tucking her black braids underneath her bonnet.

"Armand says he played almost the same game in France. They call it *lacrosse*," Cécile told her. "Let's watch."

11

The girls wandered toward the open space, where the boys had already grabbed long sticks and had begun to chase a small leather ball. They bumped shoulders roughly as each boy tried to scoop the ball into the basketlike end of his stick, hoping to toss the ball toward the goal—a small square of canvas hanging from a large, lonely tree.

Shouts went up from the adults who had gathered to watch the game. *"Merveilleux!* Armand just scored," Cécile said, clapping her hands. "Who is that boy who tried to knock him down? Is it Agnès Metoyer's brother?"

Monette shook her head and turned away from the noisy onlookers. "Didn't you hear?" she asked. "Agnès and Fanny's family left town yesterday. They're going to their uncle's plantation upriver."

Cécile shrugged. "They usually go away when it gets too hot, don't they?"

Monette leaned closer. "The Valliens are gone, too, and so are the Christophes and the Manuels— and those families *never* go away. My papa says most of his American customers have left, too." She paused and looked at Cécile with worried eyes. "They're all leaving because they're afraid of yellow fever."

Cécile's heart thumped. "Monette, do you know more?"

"*Les enfants, venez manger!*" Madame Bruiller's voice called out. "Children, come eat!"

"I'm sorry, Cécile, that's all I've heard." Monette squeezed Cécile's shoulder and dashed off to eat with her family.

Cécile dragged her feet slowly through the grass. She turned back toward the game, but it was breaking up as the Bruiller brothers left to join their family. Cécile looked at the players and the small crowd that had gathered. How many of them would still be around next Sunday? Would her newest friend, Marie-Grace, leave New Orleans, too?

Armand came up beside her, still breathless from the game. "What in the world are you frowning about?" he teased. "Didn't you see me score?"

"Nothing . . . I mean, yes!" Cécile looked up at her brother's laughing face. Everyone was crowding around him now, congratulating him. She wouldn't spoil his great day by saying that horrid word—*fever.*

CHAPTER
TWO
—

CLOUDY SKIES

After the picnic, the skies turned gray, and there were two days of rain. Cécile read a little and sewed a little, but she felt very restless. She wondered which of her friends were still in town, and what was happening in the city. When Wednesday came, dreary but dry, she eagerly agreed to go along with Tante Tay to do errands.

"It's so good to get out of the house, isn't it, chérie?" Tante Tay asked, once they were settled in the hired carriage.

"Oui," Cécile agreed. She scooted to the edge of her seat and leaned toward her young aunt. Here was a chance to ask about the troubling things she had overheard Maman and Tante Tay whispering about. What had happened when the fever spread through New Orleans before? Why was yellow fever so much worse than any other sickness? Had Maman *really* been a nurse?

"Tante Tay, I wanted to ask—" Cécile began, but her aunt was already talking.

"First, we'll make a quick stop to deliver Mathilde's gingerbread to La Maison."

Cécile nodded. La Maison was the home for elderly ladies of color. They always welcomed her warmly and begged her to recite a poem or a few lines from a play. They knew that her dearest dream was to one day become an actress, and they encouraged her every effort.

"Then we'll go to the orphanages, Children of Mercy first, then Holy Trinity."

Children of Mercy was the recently opened home for orphaned girls of color. Cécile was eager to see it, but Holy Trinity was the place that Marie-Grace had taken baby Philip!

"Will we visit for a while at Holy Trinity?" she asked hopefully. Cécile's worry about yellow fever faded for a moment as her mind filled with curiosity

15

about the baby she and Marie-Grace had rescued. How was he faring at the orphanage?

"Of course we'll visit. It's always good to see Sister Beatrice, *non*? Besides, she and I have much to catch up on," Tante Tay said. Her straw hat tilted as she turned to look out at the street.

Cécile knew that when Tante Tay was just a girl and Maman an unmarried young woman, both their mother and father had died. Sister Beatrice, then a young nun herself, had helped them a great deal, and now she was a dear friend. Now that Sister Beatrice was director of Holy Trinity, Maman and Tante Tay often brought food for the orphanage or came to tea. They always looked forward to the visits.

But today, something was different. Though Tante Tay's voice was lighthearted, Cécile studied her face carefully. *She's worried*, Cécile thought.

"Octavia! Cécile! *Entrez!* Come in, come in," Sister Beatrice greeted them at the tall green doors of the orphanage. She hugged Cécile first and then put her arm around Tante Tay.

Today more noise than usual was coming from the courtyard, where the children played. Cécile set down her basket of peaches and plums and peeked out. Her spirits rose. There, kneeling among a cluster of toddlers, was Marie-Grace Gardner!

"May I go and say hello to a friend?" she asked eagerly.

"Why, of course, my dear," Sister Beatrice said. She whisked Tante Tay into her office for tea as Cécile started toward the courtyard.

"Cécile!" Marie-Grace looked up from a lively game of pat-a-cake with a little girl and scrambled up from her knees.

"Marie-Grace!" Cécile rushed outside. "I'm so happy to see you! Why are you here? How is little Philip? Oh, I have many questions!"

"And I have so much to tell," Marie-Grace said, catching Cécile's hand. The two friends hurried to sit on a small wooden bench, each barely able to hold in her words.

"Baby Philip—is he really safe now that he's here?" Cécile began.

"Oh, he's safe," Marie-Grace reassured her. "But he's not here. He's . . . in Chicago."

17

Cécile caught her breath. "But why? That's so far away! Will you ever see him again?" She knew that her friend had grown very fond of the baby.

Marie-Grace shook her head, and her smile lost a little of its brightness. "One of the volunteers took him to an orphanage there, and he'll probably be adopted. It—it's the best thing for him. Now we can be sure that he won't get the fever."

Cécile's eyes widened. "You mean yellow fever, don't you?" she said quietly. "I've heard that it's back in New Orleans."

Marie-Grace nodded. "See that little girl I was playing with?" Cécile looked across the courtyard, and she noticed that the girl was sitting alone with a forlorn look on her face, paying no attention as other children ran by.

"The poor child just lost her parents to yellow fever," Marie-Grace said. "She came to the orphanage yesterday. So did two others. Sister Beatrice says Holy Trinity may soon be crowded with orphaned children. I'm trying to help. Is that why you're here?"

"Sister Beatrice helped my maman years ago, and now we bring food, clothing—whatever the children need," Cécile explained. She wondered how

18

long their small gifts would be enough.

"Well, right now, some of the children need cheering up," Marie-Grace said, pulling Cécile to her feet. "Come, let's play with them!"

Cécile had often handed out treats to the children, but she'd never actually played with them. She looked down at her fancy dress. Play? She certainly wasn't dressed for it.

A tiny fair-skinned boy with bare feet tugged on her skirt. Cécile nodded and turned to get her basket of fruit from the hallway.

"Non!" He pulled at her skirt again. *"Racontez-nous une histoire!"*

"Tell you a story?" Cécile asked with surprise.

"Yes, yes!" Marie-Grace grinned at her.

Cécile had never thought of showing off her acting skills here. Unable to resist this chance, she loosened the ribbon on her bonnet.

Marie-Grace clapped her hands. "Listen, everyone. My friend is going to tell a story!"

Cécile walked over to the bench. She was quickly surrounded by children chattering in French and English. They settled cross-legged on the ground and looked up at her eagerly. She was inspired to give her best performance yet.

"Let me see," she began, pretending to think hard. "Ah, I know! Once there was a little girl, and there was a wolf."

"Je ne comprends pas 'wolf,'" a small voice complained.

"You don't understand?" Cécile leaned toward the children. *"Loup.* Wolf!" She growled. The children giggled and squealed as Cécile launched into a lively, dramatic telling of "Little Red Riding Hood." When she finished, instead of applauding her, the children just ran off in many directions, laughing and imitating her "big bad wolf." Somehow Cécile didn't mind at all.

Marie-Grace is right—my story cheered them up! Cécile turned to her friend.

"You've made them smile, Cécile," said Marie-Grace. "Some of the children need that even more than they need the food and clothing you bring." Cécile flushed with pleasure at Marie-Grace's words—but what her friend said next filled her with worry. "Sister Beatrice says that Holy Trinity will have to set up a sick ward, because some of the children who've lost their parents are sick, too,"

Marie-Grace said solemnly. "She says that yellow fever is spreading fast through the city."

"*Mon Dieu*. Good heavens." Cécile took a shaky breath. "And does your father think so, too?" Marie-Grace's father was a doctor—surely he would know the truth.

"He's...he's so busy these days that I hardly see him," Marie-Grace answered softly.

Cécile wasn't sure what to say next. She felt afraid of what was happening in her city, and she felt sad for Marie-Grace, whose mother and baby brother had died some years before. If Dr. Gardner was very busy with his patients, that meant Marie-Grace must often be alone with only the housekeeper for company.

Cécile squeezed Marie-Grace's hand, and a sudden thought made her stomach drop.

"Will—will *you* be all right?" Cécile couldn't bear to add, *because Maman said that newcomers would be in the greatest danger if yellow fever spreads.*

Marie-Grace gave her a quick return squeeze and a warm smile. "Me? Of course. Remember, I was born here in New Orleans. I had yellow fever when I was little, so I'm safe now."

21

Cécile felt a rush of relief for her friend, but she wondered how many other people in her city would be in danger. She glanced up at the sky to quiet her thoughts, but dark clouds were beginning to roll above the courtyard. Marie-Grace looked up at the same time, and both girls dashed out to lead the youngest children inside.

"Here's the rain!" Sister Beatrice announced as the peppery drizzle turned into pounding drops.

Cécile stood in the hall beside Marie-Grace and shivered in the cool breeze that blew along with the rain. They watched in silence while the children buzzed behind them.

Standing there, surrounded by the orphans, Cécile wished with her whole heart that this rain could wash the children's troubles away.

C H A P T E R
T H R E E

TROUBLES
EVERYWHERE

Two weeks later, Cécile sat by the
open windows of her room, trying
to read poetry in the morning
light. August had arrived, bringing a day of sunshine
to break July's long rainy spell, but even the fine
weather couldn't lighten her spirits. She sighed and
let the tiny book fall to her lap.

More of her friends were gone now. Grand-
père had read in the newspaper that the city wasn't
letting ships dock at the levee for fear that the fever
would spread even farther. Once or twice, she'd
heard Maman and Papa speak about someone who
was ill or who had died. It seemed that this summer,
yellow fever was striking even people they knew,

people who had lived in New Orleans all their lives. Yet whenever she asked questions, they hushed her and told her not to worry. Frustrated, Cécile tried to keep herself busy by studying her lessons or joining Marie-Grace at the orphanage a few days each week.

"Miss Cécile!" Cécile looked up to see Ellen in the doorway, smiling. "Mr. Armand wants that you should sit for him again."

"Oh, oui!" Cécile hopped joyfully to her feet. Armand still hadn't completed her portrait, and she was curious to see what details would spring to life next on his canvas.

Ellen nodded. "He let me see his fine work. Such a gift he has! Come, I'll help you dress, and I'll fix your hair just as you had it last time."

Ellen had become quite skilled at taming Cécile's thick dark curls, and in no time Cécile was ready. She skipped out to the balcony.

"Here I come, *Monsieur Artiste!*" she called over the railing, laughing. Down in the courtyard, Armand waved his paintbrush.

"I want to paint you in the same morning sun as last time," he told her as she settled on her chair. "Try holding this fan."

Cécile smiled. The beautifully painted Chinese fan that Armand handed her was one Grand-père had brought back from his travels at sea. "Like this?" she asked, tapping the fan open and tilting it just so.

"Perfect. Now let me paint your hands before the light changes." Armand dabbed the long dark brush in his right hand onto the palette he held in his left hand.

"That's red paint!" Cécile said. "I'm not wearing anything red."

"Cécé, an artist sees things differently than you do."

"Hmmm..." Cécile smiled mischievously. "Monette once nibbled at a tea cake until it looked like a rabbit, and I told her so. She insisted that it was only a tea cake—but I saw a rabbit with two long ears! Do you suppose that means I'm an artist?" Cécile could hardly keep from laughing, but Armand only smiled.

Cécile guessed that he was focused on his work, and so she kept chattering without expecting him to answer. The sun grew hotter, and the morning breeze stilled. By and by, she felt a drop of sweat trickle down her neck. She wished that she could actually *use* the Chinese fan.

"Armand, *il fait chaud!*" she said, blinking. "It's hot!"

"I know," he said, pausing to frown at his canvas. He wiped the back of his hand against his forehead, and she thought she saw his hand shaking.

"Why don't we take a break?" Cécile suggested, getting up from her chair. "I will get Monsieur Artiste a drink, *non?*" She didn't wait for an answer but hurried to dip some cool lemonade from the crock Mathilde kept in the kitchen.

Mathilde glanced up from a pile of vegetables she was chopping. "And how is the great painting coming along?" she asked.

Just as Cécile opened her mouth to answer, there was a sudden clatter and crash in the courtyard.

Before Cécile could move, Mathilde leapt to the kitchen door and gave a loud, long wail. "Ayyy! *Madame!* Madame, come quickly!" she cried.

Cécile whirled around, her heart pounding.

Armand lay sprawled on the flagstones with his eyes closed. His face was wet with sweat, and Mathilde was fanning him with her big gingham apron.

From somewhere inside the house, Maman

rushed into the courtyard. Cécile could hear Ellen running downstairs from the balcony.

Maman reached Armand first. "Mon Dieu!" she gasped, dropping to her knees beside him.

Cécile's legs wobbled when she caught sight of her mother's pale, frightened face. "Maman!" she cried. "What is it? Mathilde, what has happened?"

Maman took Armand's face between her palms. "He's burning with fever. Ellen, go and fetch the doctor! Mathilde, help me get him to the sickroom."

Cécile listened, trying to blink away the tears that insisted on rolling out anyway.

Tante Tay arrived, breathless. "Aurélia?"

"Please, send for Jean-Claude," Maman murmured.

Cécile shivered. Maman never, ever bothered Papa at the shop.

Working together, Mathilde and Maman lifted Armand. Cécile watched them as they slowly and carefully carried her brother between them. She pressed herself against the low branches of a sweet olive tree so that they could pass. Not one of the grown-ups said a word to Cécile. It was as if she didn't exist.

When the courtyard was empty, she went up to the balcony. With her eyes closed, she lay in her hammock and swung it with one foot on the floor. She listened to the sounds of the house.

She could hear Maman inside, her voice still shaky, giving orders. Mathilde's steps pounded to and fro. Doors slammed. Papa's shouts rang out as he came in. Ellen answered in a fearful singsong. Then the doctor's calm words floated up the stairs. Everything became quiet.

Someone banged loudly on the front door, making Cécile jump. Her rosary beads, forgotten in the hammock, fell to the floor. She reached to pick them up.

She heard the front door open. "Sorry, no visitors!" Ellen said, her voice frightened. "We have yellow fever here."

Ellen had said it. Armand had yellow fever.

Why had this happened, Cécile wondered, just when Armand had returned to them? Would he get well? Marie-Grace had told her that this was a terrible sickness. Tears sprang to her eyes again at the thought that her dear brother would suffer.

"Hail Mary, full of grace..." Cécile began to pray, but somehow she couldn't remember the words of the familiar prayer. Her hands were shaking. Somewhere, Maman was crying. Cécile was all alone.

Then she remembered what Armand had told her. *People are afraid because no one knows what may come,* he'd said.

She tightened her fingers firmly on her beads. *I'll try not to be afraid,* she told herself. *I don't know what's coming for my family, but I'll try to be strong. For Armand.*

SMOKE AND MUSIC

Cécile felt forgotten the next morning. Ellen never came to brush her hair or lay out her clothes, so she dressed herself and René and led him down to the courtyard.

Mathilde served *pain perdu* and bananas to them for breakfast, all the while humming a slow, sad tune that Cécile had never heard before. Then Mathilde went off to boil clothes in the huge black laundry kettle at the far corner of the yard. The regular laundress had refused to come to Dumaine Street when she heard about Armand.

"Where's Maman?" René asked Cécile as he squirmed on the seat of his child-sized chair.

"Your maman is busy, and my maman is busy," she said softly. Cécile wished that Tante Tay had joined them as she always did, because then Cécile could have found out what was happening upstairs. But there was no sign of her aunt. From the breakfast table in the courtyard, she strained to make sense of the muffled conversations drifting down from the open windows.

"Ellen!" Maman called from the small sickroom. A moment later, Ellen hurried down to the court-yard, bustled past the children without any "good morning," and went into the laundry room, coming out quickly with a stack of freshly cleaned sheets to take upstairs. Soon Mathilde disappeared into the kitchen.

"Play, Cissy!" René demanded. He scooted off his chair.

Cécile chased him around the garden paths in a wild game of tag, until the heat made her too lazy to run and made René sleepy enough for a nap. Cécile carried him to the hammock Mathilde had hung between the lemon trees. She gave it a gentle push. When she was sure that her cousin was fast asleep, she ran upstairs to her room. She returned in

a moment with her doll, Amie. She was the gift that
Armand had brought Cécile from France. Amie's
golden skin, hazel eyes, and painted dark hair
were exactly the same as Cécile's, because Armand
had made her that way.

Cécile peeked at René and then went to sit on
the little stool by the gardenias, holding Amie close
to her chest.

Armand's empty easel was still standing in the
courtyard. Someone, probably Mathilde, had taken
the canvas away and neatly arranged the paints and
brushes in their cypress-wood box.

Cécile wiped away a tear and looked at Amie's
smiling china face. "There must be a way I can help,"
she said to Amie.

Mathilde stuck her head out of the kitchen
doorway and motioned with a wooden spoon.
"You can come here, Miss Cécé, and cut this okra
for supper."

Cécile didn't hesitate. For a second she thought
of what Agnès or Fanny would say about her helping
to cook. "That's maid's work!" they'd sneer. Cécile
didn't care. She would do anything to help her
family now.

Mathilde gave her a bowl of
the small green pods, along with a
clean kitchen towel, a small knife,
and a wooden chopping board.
Cécile sat on the walk in the shade
and dumped the okra onto the

towel. She trimmed the stem off each pod and sliced
it carefully on the chopping board. Then she scraped
all the slices into the bowl.

"Bonne fille, Cécé! Good girl!" Papa's voice
surprised Cécile so, she almost tipped her bowl over.
Papa was home in the middle of the day? She stared
as her father came down the stairs carrying two
large buckets. His shirtsleeves were rolled up and
his collar was open. He crossed the yard to empty
the buckets into the drain trench that ran out to the
street, and then he went himself to the water cistern
to refill them.

"Papa!" Cécile ran to him. He opened his arms.
"Why didn't you go to the shop this morning? Is
it so bad?" she whispered. "What does the doctor
say? Oh, please tell me, Papa! Is Armand going to
be all right?"

"Slow down, chérie! Listen." Papa put a gentle

hand on Cécile's cheek. Cécile felt tears well up, but she promised herself that she would not cry.

"No, I did not go to work today. Grand-père has gone in my place. He'll watch over things at work for a few days. And yes, our Armand is very sick..." Papa paused and sighed. "But doctors don't know everything. We will just have to wait to see when the fever breaks."

"Can I do something for Armand? May I see him?" Cécile asked.

Papa went back to the cistern. "Right now, you must allow Armand to rest. Your maman is taking very good care of him; she will not leave his side, not for a minute. I'll tell her you'd like to see Armand, and you continue to be strong. This evening, I'll go for a walk with you. I'll tell you what Maman says."

"*Merci,* Papa! Thank you."

Cécile watched him walk slowly upstairs carrying the two heavy buckets. Then she remembered her kitchen job. She sliced okra until there was none left.

She carried the bowl of okra to the kitchen. "I can do more, Mathilde," she said. "Whatever you need."

At sunset, Cécile and Papa slipped from their quiet house onto Dumaine Street. Papa gave her the somber news that there had been no change in Armand's condition.

They walked a few blocks in silence. Cécile noticed that many houses were dark, with their shutters fastened tight. It seemed that yellow fever had sent half the neighborhood fleeing out of town.

As they neared the square, she saw several homes with drapes of black and purple fabric nailed above their front doors. "What's that?" she asked, tugging at Papa's arm.

"It's called 'mourning crepe.' It means someone who lived in that house has died."

"Oh," Cécile said in a small voice.

She looked away from the mourning crepe, up over the rooftops. "Papa, will it rain again? It's so cloudy."

Papa shook his head. "Those aren't rain clouds," he answered. "Look!" As he pointed to a street corner two blocks away, a strong, sharp smell stung Cécile's nose.

The corner Papa had pointed out was deserted, except for a policeman who stood watching two

Cécile noticed that many houses were dark. It seemed that yellow fever had sent half the neighborhood fleeing out of town.

other men set fire to something in a barrel. Black smoke was drifting from the barrel into the air, along with the terrible smell. Similar plumes of black smoke drifted over the rooftops from other squares and streets.

Cécile took the handkerchief Papa handed her and covered her nose and mouth. "What *is* it they're burning, Papa?" she mumbled.

"It's tar, chérie. Some people think smoke from the burning tar will somehow clean the air. They believe that dirty air is what causes the fever." He led Cécile down a side street, away from the sight and smell.

"This fever is very bad, isn't it?"

"Oui." Papa looked down at her for a moment, as if judging how much to tell her. Then he continued quietly, "Many people in New Orleans—thousands of people—have yellow fever. Newcomers to the city are dying by the hundreds every day . . . Americans, Irish, Germans. Workers on the levees have taken sick. Now yellow fever is running through the whole city, and even people who have lived here all their lives are falling ill. It's the worst epidemic our city has ever seen."

Cécile carefully folded her father's handkerchief and gave it back to him. "Papa," she asked, "will all of us at home get yellow fever like Armand?"

Papa kissed the top of her head. "I hope that the rest of us will be safe, chérie. I pray that we will be safe."

He turned his head in the direction of the levees and the river, as if he could somehow see through the deepening dusk and the buildings, as if he could see even beyond the boats anchored at the docks. Cécile wondered about her father's curious, faraway expression. She squeezed his hand.

"So what did Maman say?" she asked softly.

"What? Ah, yes. I've convinced your mother to get some rest tonight. Mathilde will sit up with Armand. Maman says you may spend a few minutes with your brother when we get home."

"Let's go home right now!"

"He may not be awake," Papa warned.

"I don't care. Please, Papa. Hurry!"

"Oui, *ma petite.*"

Cécile walked as fast as she could without running. But when Papa opened the great gate to the courtyard, she did run inside. She flew up the stairs and past her bedroom, barely noticing Tante Tay dozing in her rocking chair with René on her lap.

At the doorway of the sickroom, Cécile finally stopped.

Maman was leaning over the narrow bed, pressing a damp cloth across Armand's forehead. Armand was tossing and turning, trying to throw off his covers.

Cécile went closer. "Maman?" she whispered.

"Shhh."

"I've come to sit with him."

Her mother looked tired and worried. She wore an old calico dress. She didn't speak but gave Cécile a tiny smile and blew her a kiss as she eased past.

Cécile sat down. In the candlelight, Armand's cheeks seemed thin, and his face looked a sickly yellow. *Is that where the name comes from?* Cécile wondered. Was the sickness called yellow fever because it turned people's skin that color?

"Cécé?" Armand had stopped moving. He was blinking at her.

"Yes, it's me!" she said, trying to sound cheerful.

He closed his eyes and shivered. Cécile pulled the blanket up around his shoulders.

"Armand, mon pauvre frère," Cécile murmured. "My poor brother."

"Music," Armand murmured, moving restlessly again.

Cécile frowned. She knew that sometimes fever made people imagine things. Did Armand think he was hearing music? Or perhaps he wanted to hear music? What should she do?

"Armand, *mon pauvre frère*. My poor brother. There's no—"

"Music, Cécé..." he said more loudly.

At once, she thought of the perfect song. They had known it all their lives; they sang it at Mass. Armand would remember. She gently brushed the damp hair away from his forehead and began softly: *"Ave Maria..."*

As she sang, Cécile's prayer rose clear and strong, to fill every room and every heart in the house on Dumaine Street.

MANY WAYS TO HELP

Cécile lifted the lace curtain at the parlor window and peered out. A wagon had stopped at their house. "Papa," she called. "It's Monsieur Bruiller!"

"Awwk! Papa! Papa!" Cochon ruffled his feathers and flapped his great green wings.

Cécile tossed a cloth over his cage. "Hush!" she said, running to throw open the front door. Armand had taken ill only a week ago, but it seemed like a lifetime since she'd seen anyone outside of the family.

"Richard!" Papa hurried into the parlor to greet their guest.

Monsieur Bruiller was a tall, husky man. It

wasn't until he stepped inside to shake Papa's hand that Cécile saw Monette standing shyly behind him. Cécile smiled. A friend!

Monsieur Bruiller swept off his hat and lowered his voice. "We are so sorry to hear about Armand. How is he?" His brows wrinkled in concern.

"The fever is still in him. He's very, very weak. We hope for the best," Papa answered.

Monsieur Bruiller nodded. "We're praying for him, and for you all." He cleared his throat and gestured toward the wagon outside. "The markets and shops in the city are empty now, so my brother has sent smoked meats and fresh vegetables from his farm upriver. And my sister sent two dozen jars of fig and plum preserves. There is much more food than we need, so I'm taking the rest to the nearby orphanages and the hospital."

Papa leaned to look out at the wagon and whistled. "Mon Dieu! This is from your brother and sister all the way up at Melrose?"

"Yes. They understand how badly the fever has hit us here. How is business for you? My tailor shop is shuttered. So many gentlemen have left the city, or—"

Papa cut him off before he could say the word
that Cécile knew was coming: *died.*

"I know. Business is so bad that the only
stonecutting we are doing is making grave
markers and monuments. But let's
not speak of that now," Papa said.
"Come in and have coffee with
me. It will be good to spend a little
time with a friend."

"Oui, *mon ami!"*·

Finally the fathers moved away from the door,
and Monette shyly held out a little jar of preserves
tied with a ribbon. "For you," she said, and then she
threw her arms around Cécile.

"Has it been awful? Are you afraid for Armand?"
Monette asked softly.

Cécile didn't know how to explain what the last
week had been like. One minute her brother would
seem to be at rest, and everyone would breathe a
little easier. Then he might cry out in the middle of
the night in pain, and no one could sleep. Maman
or Tante sat with him at all hours. Ellen fetched and
carried. Cécile tried to help as best she could, calming
René or bringing cups of broth or cool lemon water

from Mathilde's kitchen up to the sickroom. The Rey world was turned upside down.

"Yes," Cécile admitted. "I am afraid. But Maman reminds me that we are not the only family to suffer."

Monette touched Cécile's arm gently. "My maman said I should help Papa deliver all this food to those who need it. Will you come with me?"

Cécile's eyes brightened at her friend's kind invitation. "Will you stop at Holy Trinity? I've been helping there. Maybe we can bring some toys, too. I'm sure Maman can do without me for an hour. I'll ask her right away!"

⬦

Monette's father dropped the girls off at Holy Trinity with crates of food to unpack while he went on to the hospital. A nun Cécile didn't know showed the girls through the entrance hall of the orphanage and into the courtyard.

"I never thought there would be so many children," Monette whispered, looking down at the small basket they'd filled quickly with old toys from Cécile's house.

Cécile was shocked, too. "Mon Dieu!" she murmured. "I was here only last week, and there weren't half so many children."

She gazed around the yard as the nun hurried away. She looked to see if Marie-Grace was here somewhere, helping. All she saw were other nuns comforting crying babies and helping toddlers totter across the walks. Some three- and four-year-olds were chasing a hoop around the yard, happy as larks. But sitting on the low garden wall were other little boys and girls who looked dazed and afraid.

Right away, a lump rose in Cécile's throat. "They must have lost their parents to the fever," she said softly. Monette took a deep breath.

"Let's play with the little ones," Cécile suggested. She took Monette's hand and led her to two little girls with blond curls who were clinging to each other. Cécile smiled and clapped her hands. "Pat-a-cake, pat-a-cake, baker's man!"

When she came to the second verse, one of the little girls uncorked her thumb from her mouth and grinned. "Roll it, roll it!" she said, making a rolling motion with her arms just as Cécile was doing.

"Yes!" Cécile cried. "Now put it in a pan!"

"Mon Dieu!" Cécile murmured. "I was here only last week, and there weren't half so many children."

47

The girls laughed, and their loud shouts of "Pat-a-cake, pat-a-cake, baker's man!" drew a crowd. Even one of the older girls came over. She didn't join in, but she began to smile.

Cécile thought of Armand and the night she'd helped him by giving him music. She would do her best to comfort these children, too.

In a short while she was racing around the courtyard to escape being tagged, having as much fun as the other children were. A giggling girl pulled at Cécile's sash, and Cécile ended up sprawled on the ground, laughing. As she got up to dust herself off, she heard the voices of singing children float from the shuttered windows facing the yard. One voice, leading the others, was clear and beautiful. Cécile looked up in surprise. Marie-Grace was here!

And all of a sudden, an idea formed in Cécile's mind: Maybe Marie-Grace's father could come to see Armand. The Reys' own doctor had said there was little he could do to cure yellow fever, but maybe Dr. Gardner could help Armand get better. He was a great doctor—Marie-Grace had said so!

As Cécile looked from window to window, the singing ended. Which room had the song come from?

"Monette," she called over her shoulder, "I'll be right back!" She ran toward the French doors that seemed nearest to the sound. She stepped inside, but then looked around in confusion. The whitewashed hall looked different somehow.

A young nun peered out from a doorway down the hall. "I'm sorry. You can't come this way. These are sickrooms now."

"*S'il vous plaît*," Cécile called softly. "If you please, where was the singing coming from?"

Just then, Marie-Grace came walking down the staircase, tying the ribbons of her bonnet. She stopped short when she saw her friend.

"Cécile!" Marie-Grace's eyes were wide with concern. Her words tumbled out. "Is everything all right? You haven't been to singing lessons, and you haven't been here. I didn't know—"

Cécile spoke quickly. "It's Armand—he has yellow fever. Please, do you think your papa could come?" She stopped as hot tears wet her cheeks.

Marie-Grace's face went pale. She took Cécile's hand. "Oh, Cécile, I'm so sorry. Of course Papa will come! I don't know how soon I'll see him, because he has so many patients. But I will give him the message myself, even if I have to stay up all night to wait for him. I'll tell him to hurry!"

Cécile couldn't answer. She only nodded.

Marie-Grace gave her friend's hand a squeeze. She left Cécile standing alone in the sunny hall.

Cécile closed her eyes and hoped that Dr. Gardner would be home soon. She wiped a hand across her cheeks to dry her tears before anyone else saw them.

Cécile still felt unsettled when she got home. Ellen came into the courtyard right after her, carrying a handful of mail. Cécile thought that Ellen's steps weren't so lively today, and she seemed very pale. Still, Ellen managed a kind look.

"All these notes!" Ellen exclaimed. "To your mama and papa, from people wishin' your brother well, I guess."

Cécile walked a few steps beside her.

"How're you doin', miss?" Ellen asked. She tugged at one of Cécile's curls. "This hair is a mess! I'll take a brush to it tomorrow, I promise." Then she added gently, "You know, were it one of my brothers flat out like that, I'd be cryin' my eyes out."

"How many brothers do you have, Ellen?" Cécile asked, realizing with some shame that she had learned very little about Ellen's family during the months that Ellen had worked for them. She hadn't ever thought to ask.

"Nine! Two are up in Boston, workin' there, and the other seven are back home in County Mayo."

"Nine brothers!" Cécile was astonished.

"Aye, and me the only girl." Ellen's eyes twinkled. "My pa calls me his 'sweet angel.' We had quite a fight, tears and all, when I decided to come to America." She sorted through the letters as she talked and handed Cécile a pink perfumed note with a wink. "But I'm a headstrong girl, just like you. I had my way!"

Ellen turned to take the rest of the mail inside, leaving Cécile smiling.

Cécile turned the note over in her hands. Whose writing was it? She ripped the envelope open.

Dearest Cécile, the letter began. *Don't you miss me?*

Cécile quickly flipped the single page over to see who had signed it. Agnès Metoyer! Cécile wouldn't have expected her to write—but just now she felt quite happy to know that friends were thinking of her, even Agnès. Cécile continued to read:

> *The country is just as hot as the*
> *city. I hate the mosquitoes. There are*
> *no parties! Mama ordered me a new*
> *dress from Paris. It's even better than*
> *your blue one, with more lace and more*
> *ribbons! I'm going to a lemonade sip*
> *tomorrow, but I'm sure it won't be as*
> *much fun as mine are in New Orleans.*
> *You and Monette must be so bored*
> *while I'm away!*

Bored! Cécile crumpled Agnès's note into a ball and shook her head. Perhaps Agnès hadn't heard that Armand was sick, but certainly she knew that all of New Orleans was struggling with a terrible epidemic. How could she sound so uncaring?

Cécile thought about the concern that both Monette and Marie-Grace had shown, not just for her own family but for others, too. She was proud to call *them* friends.

"Mathilde, I'm back! What can I do to help?" she called out, going toward the kitchen. Mouth-watering smells were wafting through the door. She tossed Agnès's letter into the cooking fire.

"If Ellen is upstairs, you could set the supper table. You know how to do it?" Mathilde took a moment to fan herself with her apron.

"Of course I do," Cécile said. "Tante Octavia taught me." She went straight to the dining room, glad to have something useful to do.

Cécile opened the doors of the big mahogany buffet and looked hard at Maman's beautiful

 dishes. She had two sets. For everyday there were creamy white plates with gold trim. For special occasions there was the German china, with a colorful garden of flowers and birds in the center of each plate. Cécile moved to the everyday plates.

Just two at a time, she decided, carefully taking a pair of the heavy plates off the shelf. She placed them on the table and went back. She counted the places: Papa, Maman, Grand-père, and Tante Tay.

She and René would eat with Ellen in the courtyard or upstairs in Cécile's room, because children never sat at table. Armand would have eaten with the grown-ups, if . . .

"Cécile?" Maman called quietly from the hall.

"Yes, Maman?"

"Two things, chérie. Come to me." Cécile ran around the table, and Maman hugged her tight. The cotton of Maman's dress smelled faintly of lavender but also of vinegar from the sickroom. Cécile looked up into her mother's eyes. She wanted to ask aloud if there was any change in her brother, but she couldn't make her lips move.

"Armand is sleeping," Maman said. "We have done everything we can for him. Now we pray."

Maman cupped Cécile's face in her soft hands and kissed her forehead. Then Maman straightened and jangled something at her waist. She unhooked a small iron key.

"Here is the key to the silver drawer," she said, holding it out to Cécile.

"The silver drawer? Oh, Maman!" Cécile closed her fist around the key and its black ribbon cord. Maman's silver was her most precious wedding present. Not even Ellen was allowed to open or close the drawer.

"And set a place for yourself at the table," Maman said. "We will forget the custom from now on."

Cécile looked up with a quiet smile for the special honor that Maman had just given her. Then she scrambled back to the buffet.

"Besides," Maman added softly, "I miss my children."

At supper that evening, Grand-père did his best to cheer everyone up. As Mathilde served bowls of spicy oyster stew, he lifted a fat oyster on his spoon and began a funny story they'd heard before.

"Why, this reminds me of the time my captain put me in charge of his pearl," he said. Cécile glanced at Papa. He would usually start to laugh as soon as Grand-père started this story.

"A pearl, *mon père?*" Papa seemed distracted as he tore off the end of a *baguette*. Maybe he was wondering, as Cécile was, what was taking Maman so long to come downstairs.

"Well!" Grand-père leaned toward Cécile, who sat next to him. "The captain sent me down into the damp, dark hold of the ship, and—"

Suddenly Cécile heard running, such furious running that it seemed to come from all directions. Then Maman appeared at the hall doorway. Her face was ashen.

Papa bolted up from his chair. "Aurélia?" He sounded as if he were choking.

"He's worse, Jean-Claude!"

Just then, Mathilde burst in from the courtyard. Tears were streaming down her face. "Oh, Madame," she said. "It's Ellen, too!"

"Oh, no." Tante Tay pushed back from the table.

Grand-père became serious at once. "I'll go—"

Cécile's stomach flip-flopped. All the adults were moving, and she didn't know where to look. In the midst of the confusion, loud knocks sounded at the front door, but no one went to answer. Cécile got up and started for the door, wincing as she passed her mother sobbing in her father's arms.

Numbly, she pulled open the heavy front door. A man she'd never seen before stood there. He was tall, and his suit was rumpled. Yet the kind eyes behind his wire-rimmed glasses seemed somehow familiar.

"Cécile?" he said. "I'm Marie-Grace's father. I'm Doctor Gardner."

C H A P T E R

S I x

PRAYERS AND HOPE

Cécile had never stayed awake all night before, but she was so worried that she couldn't sleep a bit. Finally, she got up and asked Maman what she could do to help. Maman gratefully asked her to take Tante Tay's place sitting with Ellen.

Cécile slipped into Ellen's room. Silently, Tante Tay hugged her and settled her into the rocking chair near the bed. Ellen's eyes were closed, and her face looked very pale in the candlelight. Cécile suddenly realized how often Ellen had cheered her with a smile or a kind word. She swallowed hard. "We'll take good care of you, Ellen," she whispered. "Please get well."

Through the hours of darkness, Ellen tossed fitfully but did not wake. Cécile listened as Dr. Gardner walked the halls and stairs of the Reys' home with quiet authority. He dispensed both medicine from his little black bag and firm instructions from his experience.

Maman went back and forth with him from Armand's room to Ellen's. Papa sat with Armand. While René slept unknowing, Tante Tay and Grand-père carried basins of water and towels wherever they were needed. In the kitchen, Mathilde bustled at the hearth, preparing nourishing broth, chamomile tea, and cooling pitchers of ice water.

As night gave way to morning, Ellen remained feverish and restless. Suddenly she woke and turned her head on the pillow to look directly at Cécile. Her blue eyes were unusually bright.

"I have it, don't I? I have the fever," Ellen cried out.

Cécile was startled. At that moment she had been worrying about Armand. She felt guilty that she hadn't given Ellen her full attention. "Don't worry—" she began to say.

"Don't talk nonsense to me, miss. I saw Mister Armand..." Ellen's voice faded and her thoughts seemed to drift. "Did I tell you my pa calls me his angel?"

Cécile smiled sadly. "Yes, you did," she said.

Ellen clenched the sheet roughly, as if she was in pain. Cécile half rose to get help, but Ellen whispered, "Wait, Miss Cécé. Wait."

Cécile bit her lip. Ellen's cheeks were flushed, and she was trembling. "Ellen, let me get Dr. Gardner," Cécile pleaded.

"Wait!" Ellen insisted. "Do you know . . . do you know what I think?"

Cécile sat back down. "What do you think?" she replied.

"I think I will be an angel," Ellen said softly. "Angels, they're neither servant nor slave, miss. Angels are free to fly."

Cécile didn't know what to say, and her throat felt so tight she wasn't sure she could breathe. Ellen was calm for a moment, but then the pain seemed to come back, and her body jerked in the bed.

Cécile hurried onto the balcony. "Maman! Dr. Gardner! Come quickly, please!"

As if by magic, Dr. Gardner appeared on the balcony with his bag. He glanced into the room.

"Cécile, I'll take care of Ellen," he said gravely. "You may go now."

"Come downstairs, Miss Cécé," Mathilde called from the courtyard. She stood like a soldier at the bottom of the stairs, and her white kerchief shone like a lantern in the dawn. "You come with me, *petite*," she said firmly.

Slowly, Cécile walked down the steps. She felt as if she were caught in a bad dream. Mathilde sat her on one of René's small chairs and gave her coffee with chicory and lots of cream and sugar. Cécile drank the entire cup. She was bone tired, so exhausted that her arms and legs felt heavy as she moved them.

The courtyard itself was a dream place. The morning sun was beginning to cast soft shadows among the lemon trees. Somewhere not far away, a lonely *marchande* called out her song, offering cinnamon buns for sale. Cécile put both feet on the flagstone path and stood up, holding on to the table like a baby just learning to walk.

When she let go, she stepped gingerly with her bare feet across the courtyard and into the house. It was quiet. She tiptoed through the dining room and slipped into the parlor, which was still darkened by shutters that were closed against the outside.

She stopped. Someone was there, sitting in the dark. "Cécile?"

Cécile turned toward the sound of her mother's voice. "Maman?" She blinked to make sense of the shapes in the dimness. "Papa?"

Her parents were together, sitting on the velvet settee. What did it mean?

"Open the shutters, ma petite," Papa said.

Cécile's heart thumped as she crossed the room to unfasten the brass hooks. Light streamed in. She turned slowly to see her parents clearly.

Maman and Papa sat hand in hand. Maman smiled tiredly, but her eyes were shining.

"He is awake, Cécile," Maman said. "Armand is awake. The fever broke in the night, and it hasn't come back. He's hungry!"

Cécile couldn't believe what she was hearing. "He is?" she whispered. When Maman nodded, Cécile clasped her hands in joy. "He's going to get well?"

Papa rubbed the back of his neck wearily. "I had no faith in doctors, but that Dr. Gardner... Armand will recover, yes. But it will be a long time before he has the strength to cut stone."

Cécile opened her mouth, but then closed it quickly before Armand's secret slipped out.

Papa gave her a small smile. "Oh, I know about his painting. You two didn't think Monsieur Fontenot wouldn't write to me of what a fine artist my son is? When he's well enough, we'll talk, Armand and I."

Cécile rushed to give her father a kiss on the cheek. "Merci, Papa! Merci!"

Cécile's thanks were interrupted by the gruff sound of a man clearing his throat. It was Dr. Gardner, paused in the doorway.

"I have bad news," he said. Cécile froze.

Papa loosened himself from his daughter and wife and stood up.

"Ellen has died," the doctor said softly.

Papa bowed his head.

"Oh, mon Dieu. Poor Ellen," Maman moaned, thumping her lap with her fist. Cécile dropped onto the settee beside her mother.

"I'm sorry," Dr. Gardner said. Cécile could tell from the sound of his voice that he really meant it. *How can he do such difficult work?* she thought. *He must be a very brave person.*

"Armand is safe now," Dr. Gardner said. "He must take care and get plenty of rest."

"Thank you. Thank you for everything," Papa said, shaking the doctor's hand. "Please, stay and let us offer you breakfast—"

"Thank you, but I really must go." Dr. Gardner began buttoning his waistcoat.

"Coffee and a *beignet*, then. I'm sure you need something. I insist!" Papa said.

Dr. Gardner gave a small bow in Maman's direction and followed Papa out.

"Maman?" Cécile tried to steady her voice. "Did you know that Ellen had nine brothers?"

Maman's eyebrows raised in surprise. "Non," she said softly. "I knew of one brother. And I know she had parents. I'll write to them. She was a kind, hardworking girl."

Cécile curled up onto her mother's lap. She was so big now that her hair brushed Maman's chin, but she didn't care. In her thoughts, she could hear Ellen speaking. "Were it one of my brothers, I'd be cryin' my eyes out."

This time Cécile couldn't hold back her tears. She sobbed, not for her brother this time, but for Ellen.

"Try to eat more." Cécile waved a spoonful of custard temptingly in front of her brother's nose.

Armand laid his head back against his pillows and laughed. "Are you the mama bird?" he joked.

Only a few days had passed since Armand's fever had broken, and already he was teasing her again. Cécile loved it. She set the spoon back into the dish with a clink.

"No, that would be Mathilde. She'll fatten you up. You'll see!"

"Back to normal between you, is it?" Tante Tay asked, smiling as she came into the room.

"Not until he can pull my hair!" Cécile said.

Armand rolled his eyes. He was thin and very pale, and he was still too weak to get out of bed. *But he's alive,* Cécile thought gratefully as Tante Tay picked up his breakfast tray. Then another thought tumbled after: *And Ellen isn't.*

Cécile felt Tante Tay's watchful eyes on her. "Your maman says you should let the boy get some rest, chatterbox. Come downstairs with me."

Cécile waved to her brother, whose eyelids were

already drooping. He was still sleeping a lot, but Dr. Gardner had been around to say that Armand was coming along just fine.

In the parlor, Cécile found Grand-père reading the newspaper. Cochon squawked, *"Pecans, girl! PECANS!"* from his perch in the corner. Cécile dug into the pocket of her pinafore and held up a palm full of shelled pecan halves. Cochon scooped them up with his beak like the pig he truly was.

Maman sat at her writing table by the window. Her wavy black hair was pulled neatly into a bun at her neck, and her round wire glasses dangled from a velvet cord against her navy linen dress. She beckoned Cécile to join her.

"I thought you would like to know that I've written letters to Ellen's brothers in Boston and to her parents in Ireland. She had some special things— a locket and a prayer book—that Mathilde will wrap. We'll send those, too, along with her wages." Maman's dark eyes showed great emotion, yet her voice was firm and steady.

Cécile saw the quiet strength in her mother's face,

and then she looked down, pushing at the edge of the rug with her toes. Just a few weeks ago, Cécile had dreamed of a career onstage: singing, reciting poetry, acting in plays. Attention and applause were what she had wanted. In a way, even her visits to La Maison had been practice—practice for becoming famous.

None of that mattered anymore. Yellow fever had changed everything.

"We are proud of you, chérie. You were a great help during these difficult days." Maman smiled. "There is a saying: 'From those to whom much is given, much is expected.' Do you know what that means?"

Cécile looked into her mother's eyes and took a deep breath. This wasn't a test, like one her tutor, Monsieur Lejeune, might quiz her with, or a riddle to see how clever she was. Maman was talking about real life. And what had been more real for her family than this summer of sorrows?

"I think..." Cécile paused, choosing her words carefully. "I think it means that what people give us—not money or fancy clothes or such things... but things like kindness and love—we should always give to someone else?" She paused, uncertain, and then she brightened. "I mean that we should pass those gifts on to others."

Maman's eyes shone. "Surely my child has grown up," she said.

Grand-père looked over the top of his newspaper. "So true," he said. "So true."

Then he cleared his throat, and his newspaper rustled as he lowered it. "*Écoutez*. Listen," he said. "Here it says that Mayor Crossman has called for the citizens of New Orleans to go to church tomorrow, to pray for an end to this horrible epidemic. The cathedral will be open at eleven in the morning, and we shall all go. We—all of New Orleans—shall give thanks for what we have, and shed tears for what we have lost."

⁂

As Cécile stepped inside St. Louis Cathedral the next morning, the chandeliers glowed gold against the ceiling, making the brilliantly painted saints and angels seem to look down from heaven.

Suddenly Cécile remembered the last words that Ellen had said to her. Now she prayed that Ellen truly was an angel, flying free.

68

Cécile's family began walking down the aisle to find a spot in one of the wooden pews. Papa and Grand-père led the way; Cécile walked between Maman and Tante Tay. Cécile looked at the swelling crowd and was amazed at the scores of different kinds of people already seated or kneeling in prayer. She arched her neck and saw the carriage driver, Monsieur Antoine, across the aisle, looking uncomfortably stiff in a dark shirt and a red waistcoat. His face looked long and sad; maybe he had lost someone to the fever, too.

She spotted her tutor, Monsieur Lejeune, up front. Nearby were some soldiers in uniform, standing at attention. And there, on the other side of the aisle, were the two Americans who had once been so rude to Grand-père in Madame Zulime's praline shop. Suddenly Cécile's anger at them was gone as she realized the sad reason they might be here.

Cécile pulled her rosary from her pocket and began to finger the beads. The scents of candle wax, spicy incense, and women's perfumes mingled together, making the warm air heavy and hard to breathe.

Papa found a pew that was still half-empty. He went in first, then Grand-père and Maman. Cécile was about to follow when she saw a tall, well-dressed man pause by a stand of small candles near the front of the church. With him was a girl about her own age. Cécile caught her breath. It was Marie-Grace and her Uncle Luc.

"Tante Tay, come with me." Cécile clutched her aunt's arm, knowing that it would not be proper for her to leave the pew alone. "That's Dr. Gardner's daughter. I want to . . . I *must* say something to her."

Cécile tugged Tante Octavia toward the stand of candles. As they got closer, Cécile saw Marie-Grace light a candle and then kneel on the velvet cushion in front of the stand.

The joyful thanks that Cécile had been saving caught in her throat. *If Marie-Grace is lighting a candle,* Cécile realized, *that means she is offering a special prayer for someone.*

"Marie-Grace?" Cécile knelt gently beside her friend.

"Oh, Cécile." Marie-Grace wrapped her arms around Cécile. "It's Mademoiselle Océane!" she whispered.

Cécile gasped. She glanced up and saw Monsieur Luc's worried eyes. She didn't want to believe the

"It's Mademoiselle Océane," Marie-Grace whispered. Cécile gasped.
She didn't want to believe the news.

news. Mademoiselle Océane was so kind to them. And she and Monsieur Luc were getting married! Cécile knew how much Marie-Grace wanted her for an aunt. Marie-Grace's own mother had died, and Mademoiselle Océane was very kind to her.

Cécile grasped Marie-Grace's hands. What could she say to comfort her friend?

It was Tante Tay who invited Marie-Grace and her uncle to come to the pew with the Rey family. Monsieur Luc slipped in beside Grand-père. The girls sat together.

"She's so sick!" Marie-Grace whispered. "Even Papa isn't sure . . ." She couldn't continue.

"Your father is a wonderful doctor. I know he will help Mademoiselle, just as he helped Armand," Cécile said. "Thank you for sending him."

Marie-Grace nodded, wiping her eyes with her handkerchief. "I'm so glad that Armand is better. Papa told me that Ellen died. I'm sorry."

"Your father did all he could," Cécile said.

The girls knelt shoulder to shoulder, saying nothing more until the cathedral organ began to hum. The entire building echoed the instrument's majestic sounds.

Cécile lifted her rosary and saw a flicker of candlelight bounce off its beads.

"Each bead is a prayer," she said to Marie-Grace, raising her voice to be heard over the music.

"I know." Marie-Grace pulled her own rosary from the pocket of her dress. "Uncle Luc gave me one."

Cécile looked down at the small, jewel-like beads. They sparked a more hopeful thought in her mind. "I think I'll start making a beaded purse for Mademoiselle Océane—for her wedding!" She could see it already, tiny beads stitched into a beautiful pattern. "Would you do it with me? My beads will be prayer, and your beads will be hope. When we finish—"

"—she will have the most special wedding gift!" Marie-Grace's worried expression softened.

"Mademoiselle Océane will come back to us," Cécile said. "I know it!"

New Orleans will come back to us, too, she thought. She looked up at the domed ceiling, filled with angels flying, as Mass began.

LOOKING BACK

Died of Yellow Fever
SERCY,
Born Aug 29th
Died Aug 30th
MARY LOVE
Born Oct 7th
Died Aug 30th
EDWIN GIVEN
Born Dec 3rd
Died Aug 31st

THE YELLOW FEVER
EPIDEMIC OF
1853

Nuns in a New Orleans orphanage tend the sick during a yellow fever epidemic.

A terrible outbreak of yellow fever really did strike New Orleans in the summer of 1853. All across the city, families fought against illness and death, just as Cécile's family does in the story. That summer, almost 30,000 people fell ill, and 10,000 people died. "The whole city was a hospital," said one New Orleans man. Another wrote, "Never have I known such cause for sadness."

It was one of the worst *epidemics,* or outbreaks of disease, ever to strike an American city. But it was far from the only one. Today, children are familiar with vaccinations against disease, but in Cécile's time, there were no antibiotics or vaccines for illnesses such as whooping cough, scarlet fever, measles, and diphtheria *(dif-THEER-ee-uh)*, which swept in deadly waves through towns and cities. People also did not have refrigeration

The yellow fever virus was passed from person to person through the bite of a certain kind of mosquito.

and modern sewage systems to keep food and water safe. Terrible diseases such as yellow fever, typhoid *(TIE-foyd)* fever, and cholera *(KAH-ler-uh)* were passed through dirty water, spoiled food, or the bites of insects that thrived in unclean conditions. These diseases often spread like wildfire, especially in the hot summer months, and they could kill victims in days or even hours.

All of America's cities suffered epidemics. In 1793, Philadelphia—then the nation's capital—was struck by a yellow fever epidemic that killed 5,000 and forced George Washington and Thomas Jefferson to flee. In 1832, a deadly cholera epidemic brought New York City to a standstill and then swept on to Boston, Cincinnati, Philadelphia, and Baltimore. In 1918, more than 500,000 people across the country died in a flu epidemic.

When yellow fever struck Philadelphia in 1793, carriages rolled through the streets night and day to collect the dead and dying.

Until well into the twentieth century, in fact, few children grew up without losing at least one parent,

A New Orleans boy, sick in bed. Many families in the 1850s had photographs taken when family members fell ill.

sibling, or close friend to illness. Even worse, the same disease might kill several family members within a few days, just as Marie-Grace lost both her mother and baby brother in a cholera epidemic.

In Cécile's time, yellow fever was one of the most feared of all the epidemic diseases, not only because of its frightening symptoms, such as yellowed skin and eyes, but because no one knew what caused it or how to prevent or cure it.

Still, when yellow fever first appeared in New Orleans in 1853, most people weren't very worried. As Armand tells Cécile, there hadn't been an epidemic in New Orleans for several years. Each summer, a few sailors and ship passengers would arrive at the docks with yellow fever, but the disease rarely spread beyond the crowded neighborhoods where poor immigrants lived. In fact, New Orleans natives like Cécile's family believed they were very unlikely to get yellow fever. (Although they didn't know it, most had probably had

mild cases as children, which kept them safe later in life.)

But in the summer of 1853, weeks of rain created ideal conditions for mosquitoes. They carried yellow fever into every part of the city, rich and poor. That year, yellow fever affected even people who had lived in New Orleans all their lives. And it was deadlier than usual.

Many families packed their bags and fled to the countryside. Ships bringing food and supplies avoided New Orleans for fear of the fever. Business and social life came to a stop. Hospitals and orphanages overflowed. Grave diggers worked around the clock, and still coffins piled up at the cemeteries waiting for burial. Desperate to drive away whatever was causing the fever, the mayor had cannons

A sick ward in New Orleans' Charity Hospital, crowded with fever victims

fired every morning and
barrels of tar burned on
the street corners, creating
thick clouds of stinging
smoke that hung over
the city.

*During epidemics many cities burned barrels of tar,
hoping the smoke would drive away disease.*

Yet the people of
New Orleans refused to
give in to panic. For the most part, they faced the
epidemic with remarkable calm and courage. Like Cécile
and Marie-Grace and their families, those who remained
healthy turned all their efforts to caring for the sick and
the orphaned and burying the dead.

A private service group, the Howard Association,
organized efforts to get medicine, food, and medical
care to those who needed it, free of charge. The city's
doctors, like Marie-Grace's father, tended patients
night and day, and when the hospitals ran out of room,
doctors turned a ballroom into a well-
organized temporary hospital. Nurses
served heroically in homes and hospitals,
earning great respect for the fine care
they provided. Catholic nuns, who
ran many of the city's orphanages and
hospitals, also worked tirelessly to help
the sick and suffering. Often, doctors,

*Aimée Potens, one of
many nurses of color who
saved lives and eased
suffering during the
terrible summer of 1853*

80

nurses, nuns, and priests became ill themselves, and many lost their lives to the fever.

In late August, the number of deaths fell slightly, and people began to hope that the end of the epidemic was in sight. The mayor declared Friday, September 2, a day of prayer and fasting. Churches overflowed as people all across the city gathered together to grieve and to pray, just as Cécile and her family do.

By October, the epidemic of 1853 was over and the city began to come back to life. Schools and shops opened again, and more and more ships returned to New Orleans. The rest of the nation had followed the progress of the epidemic and had sent money, doctors, and supplies. Newspapers as far away as Philadelphia and Baltimore wrote of the courage and spirit with which New Orleans had faced the most devastating epidemic the nation had ever seen.

This New Orleans cemetery was established in 1854. It was needed because so many people had died of yellow fever the year before.

Glossary of French Words

baguette *(bah-get)*—a loaf of French bread

beignet *(beh-nyeh)*—a puffy fried bread, similar to a square doughnut

bonjour *(bohn-zhoor)*—hello

bonne fille *(bun feey)*—good girl

C'est vrai. *(say vray)*—It's true.

chérie *(shay-ree)*—dear, darling (used for a girl or woman)

Écoutez. *(ay-koo-tay)*—Listen.

Entrez! *(ahn-tray)*—Come in!

grand-père *(grahn-pehr)*—grandfather, grandpa

Il fait chaud. *(eel feh shoh)*—It's hot.

je ne comprends pas *(zhun kohm-prahn pah)*—I don't understand

lacrosse *(lah-krohss)*—a game similar to field hockey

Les enfants, venez manger! *(layz ahn-fahn, vuh-nay mahn-zhay)*—Children, come eat.

loup *(loo)*—wolf

madame *(mah-dahm)*—ma'am, Mrs.

mademoiselle *(mahd-mwah-zel)*—Miss, young lady

maman *(mah-mahn)*—mother, mama

ma petite *(mah puh-teet)*—my little one

marchande *(mar-shahnd)*—female seller or merchant

merci *(mehr-see)*—thank you

merveilleux *(mehr-veh-yuh)*—marvelous, wonderful

mon ami *(mohn ah-mee)*—my friend

mon Dieu *(mohn dyuh)*—good heavens; my God

mon pauvre frère (*mohn poh-vruh frehr*)—my poor brother

mon père *(mohn pehr)*—my father

monsieur *(muh-syuh)*—sir, Mr.

Monsieur Artiste *(muh-syuh ar-teest)*—Mr. Artist, Sir Artist

non *(nohn)*—no

oui *(wee)*—yes

pain perdu *(pen pehr-dew)*—French toast

petite *(puh-teet)*—little one

Quelqu'un écoute. *(kel-kun ay-koot)*—Someone's listening.

Racontez-nous une histoire! *(rah-kohn-tay-noo ewn ee-stwar)*—
   Tell us a story!

raquettes *(rah-ket)*—a ball game that was popular in Louisiana,
   similar to lacrosse or field hockey

s'il vous plaît *(seel voo pleh)*—please; if you please

tante *(tahnt)*—aunt

très gentil *(treh zhahn-tee)*—very nice

How to Pronounce French Names

Agnès Metoyer *(ah-nyess meh-twah-yay)*

Amie *(ah-mee)*

Antoine *(ahn-twahn)*

Armand *(ar-mahn)*

Aurélia *(oh-ray-lya)*

Cécé *(say-say)*

Cécile Rey *(say-seel ray)*

Christophes *(kree-stohf)*

Cochon *(koh-shohn)*

Fontenot *(fohn-tuh-noh)*

Jean-Claude *(zhahn-klohd)*

La Maison *(lah meh-zohn)*

Lejeune *(luh-zhuhn)*

Luc *(lewk)*

Mathilde *(mah-tild)*

Monette Bruiller *(moh-net brew-yay)*

Océane *(oh-say-ahn)*

Octavia *(ohk-tah-vyah)*

Pontchartrain *(pohn-shar-tren)*

René *(ruh-nay)*

Richard *(ree-shar)*

Valliens *(vah-lyen)*

Zulime *(zew-leem)*

GET THE WHOLE STORY

Two very different girls share a unique friendship and a remarkable story. Cécile's and Marie-Grace's books take turns describing the year that changes both their lives. Read all six!

Available at bookstores and at *americangirl.com*

BOOK 1: MEET MARIE-GRACE
When Marie-Grace arrives in New Orleans, she's not sure she fits in—until an unexpected invitation opens the door to friendship.

BOOK 2: MEET CÉCILE
Cécile plans a secret adventure at a glittering costume ball. But her daring plan won't work unless Marie-Grace is brave enough to take part, too!

BOOK 3: MARIE-GRACE AND THE ORPHANS
Marie-Grace discovers an abandoned baby. With Cécile's help, she finds a safe place for him. But when a fever threatens the city, she wonders if *anyone* will be safe.

BOOK 4: TROUBLES FOR CÉCILE
Yellow fever spreads through the city—and into Cécile's own home. Marie-Grace offers help, but it's up to Cécile to be strong when her family needs her most.

BOOK 5: MARIE-GRACE MAKES A DIFFERENCE
As the fever rages on, Marie-Grace and Cécile volunteer at a crowded orphanage. Then Marie-Grace discovers that it's not just the orphans who need help.

BOOK 6: CÉCILE'S GIFT
The epidemic is over, but it has changed Cécile—and New Orleans—forever. With Marie-Grace's encouragement, Cécile steps onstage to help her beloved city recover.

A SNEAK PEEK AT
THE NEXT BOOK IN THE SERIES

Marie-Grace

MAKES A DIFFERENCE

Marie-Grace Gardner looked around the noisy courtyard of Holy Trinity Orphanage. *Where is Cécile?* she wondered. She and her friend were both volunteers at the orphanage. They were supposed to meet this morning, but Cécile had not yet arrived—and she hadn't sent a message, either. Marie-Grace was starting to worry when she saw her friend hurrying across the orphanage courtyard.

"How is Armand?" Marie-Grace asked anxiously.

"He's much better, thank you," Cécile answered breathlessly. "I'm sorry I'm late—Maman needed my help filling baskets for the sick. What have you heard about Mademoiselle Océane? Is she better?"

"I don't know," admitted Marie-Grace. Despite the heat of the day, she felt a chill of fear. "I keep hoping for news from Uncle Luc, but I haven't heard anything since I saw you at the special day of prayer."

"I'm sure your uncle is with Mademoiselle," Cécile reassured her. "My maman hardly left Armand for a moment when he had the fever. And we all took turns sitting with Ellen, too, until . . . " Cécile did not finish her sentence.

The girls were both silent for a moment. Marie-Grace understood how terrible sickness could be. Four years ago, her mother and her baby brother, Daniel, had died in a cholera epidemic in New Orleans. Soon afterward, Marie-Grace and her father had left the city. They'd spent several years moving around the Northeast, but they had never found a true home. Marie-Grace had been glad when she and Papa returned to New Orleans in January. But once again, it seemed as if sickness was threatening her whole world—and her friend's world, too.

Marie-Grace touched Cécile's arm. "I'm very sorry about Ellen," she said gently.

"I can't believe she's gone," Cécile said sadly. Then she looked at Marie-Grace with fierce determination. "We have to find some way to help Mademoiselle Océane."

"I've been thinking that, too," Marie-Grace agreed. "But I don't know what we can do."

"There must be *something*," Cécile persisted. "What does your papa say?"

Marie-Grace tried to think of how to answer. Cécile had a big, loving family, and she always had lots of people to talk with. Marie-Grace wondered how she could explain to her friend that, for the last few weeks, she'd hardly seen Papa at all. He had been too busy taking care of yellow fever patients.

"Papa works every day from early in the morning till late at night," Marie-Grace said at last. "He doesn't have much time to talk."

Cécile nodded. "He stayed at our house all night taking care of Armand. He has many patients to visit, doesn't he?"

"Yes," said Marie-Grace, thinking of how tired her father had looked that morning. "And all he said about Mademoiselle Océane is that we should pray for her. I think Papa's worried."

Ding! Ding! Clanging filled the court-yard. Sister Beatrice was ringing the bell to announce the midday meal. The children gathered at a big basin  in the corner to wash their hands and faces before rushing inside.

"I'm glad you girls are here to help," Sister Beatrice told Marie-Grace and Cécile as they followed the children into the dining hall. "We've had twenty-seven new children arrive this week. That's more than we usually have in a year."

So many orphans! thought Marie-Grace as she tied an apron around her waist. Children ranging in age from toddlers to five-year-olds sat crammed together on the benches. Many squirmed eagerly as they waited for their dinners.

Sister Beatrice handed Marie-Grace and Cécile baskets of delicious-smelling warm bread. "If there is any extra, give it to the new children," she said quietly. "Some of them haven't had much to eat in a long time."

"Yes, Sister," the girls said together. Food was getting harder to find in the city. Some of the ships that brought supplies to New Orleans were now avoiding the port because of the fever. There were empty stalls in the markets, too, and many bakeries and shops were closed because their owners had fled the city.

"We'll make sure everyone gets enough," Marie-Grace promised.

For the next hour, she and Cécile passed out bread and scooped red beans and rice from big iron pots. When the meal was over, the orphans stayed inside for their afternoon rest. Marie-Grace and Cécile went outside and sat under the shade of a magnolia tree at the far end of the courtyard.

Cécile took a flask of lemonade, some bread, and several plump figs from her basket. "Aren't you going to eat something?" she asked Marie-Grace.

Marie-Grace shook her head. She was so worried about Mademoiselle Océane that it was hard to think about eating. Even though Mademoiselle was not yet her aunt, she had treated Marie-Grace like a favorite niece. Marie-Grace remembered the many happy times they'd had together, singing, talking, and sipping tea.

What if Mademoiselle doesn't get better? worried Marie-Grace. Her stomach twisted in a knot when she considered the possibility. *It would almost be like losing Mama all over again,* she realized.

"I'm not hungry," she told Cécile.

Cécile didn't seem surprised. "When Armand was sick, I forgot to eat sometimes," she said as she tore her bread in half. "But Maman said I had to stay strong so that I could help Armand. And I did help him. I sang to him when he was sick, and it made him feel better." Cécile handed half her bread to Marie-Grace. "Here, you have to stay strong if you're going to help Mademoiselle."

92

Cécile handed half her bread to Marie-Grace.
"You have to stay strong if you're going to help Mademoiselle."

The bread felt dry in Marie-Grace's mouth, but Cécile insisted that she have some figs, too. After a few bites of food and a long drink of lemonade, Marie-Grace began to feel a little better.

Cécile picked up a late-blooming magnolia flower that had fallen on the ground. "Look at this," she said, holding up the sweet-smelling blossom. "Wouldn't it be perfect for Mademoiselle's wedding?"

There may not even be a wedding now, Marie-Grace thought. But she couldn't bring herself to say those words aloud.

"I think I have an idea for how we could help Mademoiselle," Cécile said slowly.

Marie-Grace sat up straight. "You do?"